The Iron Ship

Stories linking with the History
National Curriculum Key Stage 2

First published in 1999 by Franklin Watts
96 Leonard Street, London EC2A 4XD

Franklin Watts Australia
56 O'Riordan Street, Alexandria, Sydney, NSW 2015

This edition published 2002
Text © Dennis Hamley 1999

Editor: Sarah Snashall
Designer: Jason Anscomb
Consultant: Dr Anne Millard, BA Hons, Dip Ed, PhD

A CIP catalogue record for this book
is available from the British Library.

ISBN 0 7496 4605 5 (pbk)

Dewey Classification 941.081

Printed in Great Britain

The Iron Ship

by
Dennis Hamley
Illustrations by Martin Remphry

W
FRANKLIN WATTS
LONDON•SYDNEY

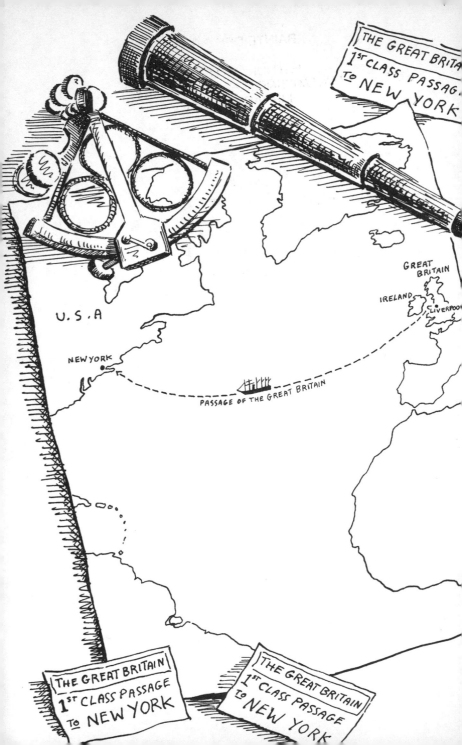

1
Aground!

Wilbur Wanthrop II woke suddenly. For a second he couldn't work out where he was. Terrifying sounds crashed into his ear. He heard metal plates squealing and straining, a loud clanging noise which echoed as if a blacksmith was trying to hammer a way

through iron, a weird grinding noise as if a giant's teeth were trying to bite into the floor beneath. He felt a mighty juddering all round and the walls and ceiling shook as if they were about to fall to pieces. The world must be coming to a violent end.

Then he remembered. He was lying in his bunk in his parents' first-class stateroom on the *Great Britain,* the new steamer built by Mr Brunel for the transatlantic run. Before he slept, he had been getting used to the ship's movement in the light swell of the Irish Sea, the thrumming of the hull's iron sides and the steady beat of the huge steam engines. Hours before, he had dozed off very happy. So what terrible thing was happening now?

★ ★ ★ ★

Wilbur was twelve. He had left New York with his parents on the first voyage back to Liverpool the *Great Britain* ever made.

That was a year ago now. Today, September 22nd, 1846, they were returning. Trust his father, Wilbur Wanthrop I, to insist on crossing the Atlantic on the newest, biggest, fastest ship in the world, the first made entirely of iron instead of wood and the first big steamer to be driven by a screw propeller rather than paddle wheels. "That Brunel guy, he sure knows what he's about," he had said. "He thinks more like a Yankee than a Limey."

Whether he did or not, young Wilbur knew all about the great Isambard Kingdom Brunel – his wonderful bridges, superb railways, so much faster and more comfortable than anyone else's, and now his great steamships. Why, the *Great Britain* could cross the Atlantic from New York to Liverpool in thirteen days – no other ship could go nearly as fast. That voyage from America had been the greatest time of Wilbur's life.

The year which followed, as the Wanthrops toured Europe, had been nothing by comparison. The sights of the old continent – London, Paris, Rome, Berlin, Vienna – had left him cold. Heading home on the *Great Britain*, he felt truly happy. One hundred and eighty passengers were on board – never had so many people crossed the Atlantic together. This would be a historic voyage which he would never forget.

* * * *

Wilbur sat up. The great ship suddenly lurched to one side. Wilbur found himself falling out of bed. He scrambled up off the floor, trembling with fear. He could hear

running feet outside and the air was filled with cries of 'Shipwreck!', 'God save us all!' and 'We're lost!'

Suddenly his parents were standing over him, his mother crying and comforting him, "Everything will be all right, Wilbur. Pray to the Lord and he'll see us through."

"I must go and see what's happening," said Wilbur, and before they could stop him he was out on deck, with cold salt spray from the breaking waves wetting his face. Wilbur could hear the roar and hiss of engines being shut down and coal thrown overboard, he saw the flash and flare of signal guns. A distraught man beside him shouted, "We'll die. No ship can stand this pounding."

"This one can," answered Wilbur, "I've read how Mr Brunel built it. The *Great Britain* can put up with anything."

A loud voice sounded above the rabble. Captain Hosken was regaining order through his megaphone. "Ladies and gentlemen,

please be calm. This ship will not break up. You are completely safe. Please go back to your cabins until morning. We hope to float off at high tide."

"Where are we, Sir?" enquired a voice.

"I believe we are aground on the northern tip of the Isle of Man," Captain Hosken replied.

Calmed by his strong, confident voice, the passengers left for their cabins. Tomorrow, they would float off and perhaps be on their way, with but a few hours delay.

The Wanthrops climbed back into their bunks and were soon soundly asleep, even

though the floor was listing by several degrees
to one side.

★ ★ ★ ★

Dawn broke and the sun rose. Captain
Hosken and his officers, the rest of the crew
and all the passengers stared at the sight.

The *Great Britain* was stuck fast,
canted at an angle on wet sand where the
tide was running out. To the north were low
green fields. To the south, the sands of a
huge bay stretched for miles until, far away,
a range of mountains, steep, high, awesome,

swept down to the shore. Wilbur could see a lone, tiny figure on the sand.

Captain Hosken shouted to his first officer. "Get a ladder over the side and tell the officers to go ashore and get help."

As Wilbur watched, the tiny figure suddenly turned and ran back towards the far-away fields where sheep and cattle grazed.

So, this was the Isle of Man.

No, it was not. A sailor looked over the rails, at the fields and mountains. "I've known this place all my life," he said. "Those are the Mountains of Mourne. We're in Dundrum Bay in County Down in Ireland."

2

Get us out of here!

Maeve loved the early mornings when the tide was going out. She had the whole of the bay to herself as she looked for mussels below the surface of the wet sand. Every morning it was so – except this one.

Even while she was still in the fields she

could see the black shape, like a monstrous log, lying across the sands. At first she was frightened. Whatever this thing was, she wouldn't go too near. Soon her bare feet felt the suck of the sand beneath them. She put down her bucket and looked more carefully.

The shape was further away than she thought. Which meant it must be much larger. It looked like a gigantic boat. But no boat was ever that big. She plucked up courage to go nearer.

Yes, it *was* a boat – but not like any boat she had seen before. A golden coat of arms flashed in the morning sunlight on the bows of the vast black hull. There were six masts with rigging for sails, and a tall black chimney. Lines of people were looking over the sides. How could so many crowd onto one ship without it sinking under their weight? And what was it doing here in the bay?

Somebody threw a ladder over the side of the boat and men climbed down. Maeve didn't wait. She ran back to the farm as fast as she could to warn her parents and brothers. Soon there was grass, not sand, under her feet. She stopped and took a last look at the great ship. Three men in dark uniforms were crossing the sands after her. She didn't hesitate. She turned and started running.

A loud cry carried towards her. "Girl! Wait there a moment. We won't hurt you."

Something about that voice made her stop again. It didn't sound like the voice of one who meant her harm. She turned back and the three sailors came nearer.

"My girl," said the first sailor. "We're in a dreadful pickle and we need your help." There were two gold rings on each sleeve of his coat and he wore a peaked cap with a white top.

"*My* help?" Maeve replied doubtfully.

"Yes, indeed. We have a hundred and eighty souls on board who thought they were going to America. They're all tired and frightened, and some of them are extremely angry."

"But how could I help?" she said.

"You're not the only one to live round this bay, surely," said the first sailor.

"No. There are farmers, like my father and brothers and there are villages nearby."

"Then we must enlist the help of everyone in getting the passengers off."

"We'll have to be quick," she said. "It's not long now before the tide turns again."

★ ★ ★ ★

3
Rescued

Maeve's father was the first out with horse and cart across the sands to take off complaining passengers. Maeve led the sailors to the next farm, and the next, then into the villages. Word spread and soon there seemed to be a never-ending stream of carts carrying

richly-dressed passengers who sat on their
luggage and held their noses in the air. The
carts' wheels sank deep in the sand and the
poor horses and donkeys had to strain and
heave to pull the huge weights.

When the last passengers were off the
Great Britain, Maeve went back to the farm
where something exciting was happening in
the kitchen.

From outside, she heard strange voices.
The accents sounded odd – somehow Irish,
and yet not. Definitely not English. What
was it?

She opened the door in time to hear a large, strange man say to her mother, "Well, Ma'am, I guess we must express our gratitude to you for your kindness and see it as adding to the debt the United States owes to the good old Emerald Isle."

A strange lady murmured, "That's right, Wilbur," but a boy about Maeve's own age turned as she entered and whispered to her, "Pa can be really pompous when he tries."

They were all drinking mugs of hot tea and eating freshly-baked soda bread spread with farm butter. When they had finished, the boy turned to

the strange woman and said, "Mom, can I go outside so this girl can show me the farm?"

"Yes, if she wants to show you," the woman replied. "But don't get yourself dirty. All your clothes are packed in the trunks."

Maeve was amazed. Boys were supposed to be shy and tongue-tied in her presence. All those who lived round the bay

were, anyway. Still, why shouldn't she show
him the farm if he asked?

She looked at her own mother, who very
slightly nodded.

So they went outside together and she
showed him the hens running round the yard,
the styes where pigs rooted, the barn where
the cows were milked, the stable for the horse.
For the first time in her life, she felt ashamed
about the mud and dung all over the ground

and winced as he walked blithely through it all in his smart breeches and shiny shoes. But he didn't seem to mind a thing.

As they went, he said his name was Wilbur, like his father's, and he lived in New York, and then he told her all about America and their tour of Europe, and especially about the *Great Britain,* and how while everybody else on the ship was grumbling about how they'd never sail on such a thing again, he knew that no other vessel would survive running aground like that, and it only showed that Mr Brunel was the greatest engineer the world had ever seen.

All this came out in a great rush and when Wilbur stopped to draw breath, she said, "But the ship's stuck. It will never sail again."

"Of course it will. The crew will throw everything heavy overboard and when the tide rises it will float off. There's no damage at all. It's resting on sand. We'll be on our way again tomorrow."

"But there *will* be damage," said Maeve. "Everybody knows there are terrible rocks just under the sand. They've torn the bottoms out of many ships over the years."

Wilbur stopped. "Last night, I remember, I heard a terrible noise. A weird

grinding roar underneath. It must have been because the rocks were tearing it open and not even iron could hold out against them. So perhaps you're right after all, Maeve."

"And now the ship will have to stay there because there'll be no tides high enough for anything that size to float until Spring comes next year, and the winter storms will pound it to pieces, just like they have every boat that's ever been caught in the bay."

"It won't. The *Great Britain*'s not like other ships," said Wilbur.

"We'll see," said Maeve.

Wilbur thought for a moment. "No, I won't see, but you will. Gee, you're lucky." He looked sad. "Say, would you write to me and tell me what's going on in the bay and how the *Great Britain* is faring."

Maeve wasn't sure, but she didn't like to refuse.

"Well, all right, but you'll have to write first" she said, thinking he would never write to her.

"OK. It's a deal." said Wilbur. OK? What did that mean? He seemed to be agreeing to her suggestion.

Now what would she do? She could read and write because she went to the little school run by the priest. But could she write to someone she hardly knew, who lived on the other side of the world?

He seemed to know what she was thinking. "I don't mind how short your letters are," he said. "Just let me know what's happening."

"OK," she answered.

4
Letters across the Atlantic

That night, Wilbur and his family were
taken to a hotel in Belfast, and the day after
they caught ship to Liverpool.

That's the end of him, Maeve thought.

But not long before Christmas a letter
arrived, written at the end of October.

Park Avenue
New York
October 28th, 1846

Dear Maeve,

Did you think that I would not write?
A Wanthrop is as good as his word.

We reached Liverpool and waited for
a passage back to New York. I wanted us
to go to Bristol and cross on the first
steamship Mr Brunel built, the Great
Western, but Pa said he was finished with
Mr Brunel, so we returned on the Britannia,
which is sailed by the Cunard Line.

We returned safely home, but the
Britannia is a poor thing compared with the
Great Britain, of no size at all, driven by
old-fashioned paddles and so slow that the
voyage took sixteen days.

Perhaps, one day, I will travel again
on one of Brunel's great ships.

Your friend,

Wilbur

Maeve read this letter with a sinking heart. How could she reply to such smooth words, sounding as if he was there talking to her? And what could she tell him?

Well, there was quite a lot. A new captain had come out from England and tried to float the ship off. But it had been no use, so he had hoisted the sails and let the wind force it further up the shore.

Then, two experts in saving ships arrived. They built great breakwaters out of wood to protect the hull, but as fast as they built them, winter storms rose up and huge waves rushed in and carried them away. After that, nobody had come near at all.

The ship lay half on its side, its bottom holed, forlorn, rusting, a sad sight which made her want to cry. Would Wilbur want to hear any of that? No. It would make him sad. So how could she answer his letter?

She felt as forlorn as the ship looked as she wandered over the bay at low tide the next day.

Nobody else ever shared her vigils on the sands. Yet today, someone was there. A man was walking across the beach, towards the ship. From a distance he looked very odd. He wore a black coat and a

stove-pipe hat which looked like the funnel on the boat behind him. His trousers were rucked up over his black shoes and both were discoloured with wet sand. He was not tall and he did not look burly or muscular, yet Maeve felt that he was very strong – his strength must be in his mind and character. Strangely, though, he seemed ready to cry.

"Are you all right, Sir?" she asked.

"Look," he answered bitterly. "The finest ship in the world, lying there like a useless saucepan. And nobody's given any more thought to protecting her than if she were a saucepan lying on Brighton beach."

"Lots of people have tried," Maeve said timidly, "I've watched them. But everything they've done has been washed away."

"They're all fools," he answered. "They do things the way they've been taught to and don't have a sensible or new thought in their heads. This isn't a wooden sailing ship. It's a steamer made of iron – the biggest in the world. But they can't see further than their noses. The ship needs to be protected from the winter storms." He paused, then looked down to Maeve. The bitterness had left his face. "What would *you* do to protect my fine ship, my child."

His fine ship? "Are you Mr Brunel?"

"Of course I am. And who are you?"

When Maeve had told him, he said, "Now I know who you are, Maeve, you can answer my question. What would you do?" Maeve was tongue-tied. "Come now, child. Don't be afraid."

"Well," Maeve started doubtfully. She didn't want to say something stupid, "I think I'd build a big fence all round it."

Mr Brunel laughed.

"My girl, you've hit on the very plan which was in my mind. If you think straight, it becomes obvious. Though we need to make sure that this fence, once we've built it, does not shift in the sand."

"How will you do that?" asked Maeve.

"I'll make a skirt of hundreds of posts tied together and bound tight round the ship with chains. I'll have it weighed down with iron weights and sandbags. If the sea washes it away, I'll have it built thicker, with even more weights. If the first doesn't work, I'll have it made ten times greater. If hundredweights won't keep it down, we must try tons. Then, when the spring tides come, we can pull them all off and the ship will float again."

He peered out towards the great ship once again. "I've seen all round her. I know she's still straight and true because I built her to be. The damage is easily and cheaply repaired. I'll round up the workmen and tell

them what's to be done. Goodbye, Maeve, and thank you."

He turned away and walked quickly back towards Dundrum.

That night, Maeve found some paper and a pen, sat at the kitchen table and, by the light of the oil lamp, began to write.

Dundrum
December 16th, 1846

Dear Wilbur,
Today I met Mr Brunel and we talked together about how we could save his ship ...

5
Saving the ship

In February, Wilbur's next letter came.

Maeve was a little bit surprised. For weeks after her letter had gone, she kept saying to herself, *He won't believe me. He'll think I made it up and that I never saw Mr Brunel at all.* But he *did* believe her.

Park Avenue,
New York
January 12th, 1847

Dear Maeve,

How I wish I was in your shoes. To be able to speak to the great man himself – how proud you must have felt. And to hear him say that what you thought he should do was exactly what he was going to do – that would be music to anybody's ears.

New York still misses the sight of one of Mr Brunel's ships entering the harbour. But one day they will return.

Your true friend,
Wilbur

Maeve had no worries about what to write now. So much had happened. The captain had come over from England again, there was furious activity in the woods and forests round about, and her father and many others had earned good money carrying bundles of cut wooden spars endlessly over the sand to where the work went on.

Teams of sailors worked to lash the spars together and weigh them down. But at first it was no use. Heavy seas washed them away as soon as the weights were in place.

"It's hopeless," everybody said. But
Maeve remembered Mr Brunel, "If
hundredweights won't keep them down, then
we must try tons." She watched as more and
more bundles of spars were lashed and
chained round the ship, more and more
weights put on to keep them down and more
and more sand fetched up against them and
held them in place. By the time Wilbur's letter
arrived, the *Great Britain* had almost
disappeared behind a great fence of wood

and sand. Now the storms could rage and the waves could pound, yet nothing more could happen to the wonderful ship.

She sat down that night and started writing again. *Dear Wilbur, So much has happened since my last letter to you ...*

★ ★ ★ ★

May came, with calmer weather and higher tides. Now it was time to try and move the ship. But things did not seem to be going well.

One day, when the sun shone and a fresh breeze scudded across the bay, Maeve found a man looking at the *Great Britain* from exactly the same place as she had found Mr Brunel the year before.

He turned and saw her. "I know you," he said. "The young collector of mussels. And your name, if I'm not mistaken, is Maeve."

"How do you know?" she asked.

"I'm Captain Claxton. Mr Brunel told me about you. And he also told me this skirt

of wood was your idea as well as his. Well,
let me tell you, I wish you'd never thought of
it. The sand has piled up around it and
hardened, and now the whole thing is a mass
more difficult to move than granite rock."

Maeve felt almost guilty. "What are
you going to do?" she asked.

"Don't worry. The skirt has done its
work. The ship is unharmed underneath,
except for the holes in the bottom. We'll
manage."

★ ★ ★ ★

In June another letter came from Wilbur.

Park Avenue,
New York
May 11th, 1847

Dear Maeve,

    Have you any more news about our great ship? Has your idea of the wooden skirt worked and saved the ship?

    I have talked about it with Pa and he says the ship is a goner. He doesn't think that even Mr Brunel can beat the powers of nature when there are such winds and storms. Nobody should have tried to build a ship like that to start with, unless he built it in America. But I tell him to trust Mr Brunel, because when you see the Great Britain, you see the ship of the future. Well, that's what I think, anyway.

    Oh, Maeve, wouldn't it be just swell if we could meet again one day?

    Your true friend,

        Wilbur

Yes, it would be lovely to meet again one day. But that would never happen. She felt as unhappy about that as she was feeling about the *Great Britain.* Once again, things were not going well. The skirt had at last been removed. As Captain Claxton had said, the hull was unharmed underneath, straight and true as when it was built. But this year, the tides just did not seem high enough to float the ship off. All through June, July, into August – even though, to make the ship lighter, everything had been taken out so there was only the hull left – still it could not float.

August was nearly gone. Surely the ship would not have to settle into the sand for another winter? There were probably not enough trees left in County Down to make another skirt.

Then, at last, on August 27th, the tide rose high and strong. The *Great Britain* rose with it. A rope was put aboard, temporary repairs were made to the bottom and, so slowly, so carefully, the ship was towed out into the bay, where two ships of the Royal Navy were waiting to take over the towing to Liverpool.

But nothing happened. What disaster had befallen the ship now?

6
Back home

The *Great Britain* was still in danger. In spite of the repairs, water was still pouring through the holes in the bottom made by the rocks. This led to arguments, even in Maeve's house.

Her father was shouting. "You've no right to leave the farm when there's work to be done." Michael and Patrick, Maeve's brothers, looked stubborn.

"Sure, and it won't be for more than a day or two, until that ship's empty of water and they can tow it back to England," said Michael.

"And wouldn't the money be grand?" said Patrick.

"Then mind you're back when you say you'll be," her father said grumpily.

"What's happening?" Maeve asked.

"They want a big gang on board to work the pumps, and we're in it," Michael answered. "They've had to take the engines out to make her light enough to float."

Maeve was full of envy. "You mean you're going on board the *Great Britain*?" she said. "I wish I could come with you."

★ ★ ★ ★

But some days passed before she could write to Wilbur again.

Dundrum Bay
September 25th, 1847

Dear Wilbur,
Today, the Great Britain *left Dundrum Bay. At last they managed to pump enough water out of her. But my brothers tell me it is still six feet deep in the engine room. Two Navy ships towed her away. I felt very sad when I saw her disappear round the headland for the last time. I felt as though everything exciting went with her and nothing good will ever happen here again. A few days later, news came that she was safely at home and we all felt very happy.*
Your friend,
Maeve

Many years passed. The old century ended, the new one began. The year was 1912. In a big house in New York, an old man was reading his newspaper. One item caught his eye. He called to his wife.

"See here, Maeve, how progress moves on. The biggest, fastest, most comfortable, safest ship ever built is sailing to New York.

Where have we heard that before? One week to go and that wonderful ship will arrive and we'll be there to see it when it docks."

Maeve looked at him fondly. "You've always loved the big steamships, haven't you, Wilbur," she said.

"It was the first ever big steamship which brought us together," Wilbur replied. "Though how tiny and crude it seems now. I envy those people setting sail from Southampton. Nothing like that can possibly happen to them. Not on the *Titanic* ..."

★ ★ ★ ★

Steam ships across the Atlantic

The *Great Western*

While Brunel was building the Great Western
Railway, someone asked whether the huge distance
between London and Bristol was not too long for
one railway. Brunel answered, "Why not make it
longer, and have a steamboat go from Bristol to
New York and call it the *Great Western?*" Some
people thought he was mad, but others realised
what a wonderful idea it was. As soon as the
railway line was complete, he set about the task
and the steamship *Great Western* was the result.

The first steamships

When the first steam engines were made, it took a long time for people to realise there could be another way besides sails to power a ship. However, the first proper steamship was built long before the first proper railway engine. The *Charlotte Dundas* was built in 1802 on the River Clyde. Soon, steamships were crossing the Channel and now attention passed to the oceans. Could a steamship ever give a regular service to America?

The *Great Britain*

All previous steamships crossing the Atlantic had been wooden paddle steamers. Brunel saw that to have screw propellers instead of paddle wheels, and iron hulls instead of wooden ones, would be far  better in every way. The *Great Britain* was as big an advance in its day as Concorde, space travel or virtual reality has been in ours. But Wilbur waited in vain for it to sail again to New York. After its disastrous running aground in Dundrum Bay, it never crossed the Atlantic again. The Great Western Steamship Company was broke. They had to sell their two great ships and the next job for the *Great Britain* was keeping up a service to Australia. Then it was sold again and ended up as a hulk used for storage in the Falkland Islands.

Brought home

In 1970 the *Great Britain* was brought home – still completely undamaged – and is now permanently

CROSS-CHANNEL FERRY

GREAT BRITAIN

on show in Bristol, where you can see it today. How small it seems now – smaller than most cross-channel ferries. But in 1846 it looked a monster, and every ship since has been built in the way Brunel first used with the *Great Britain*.

Running aground

How anybody could make such a mistake as to think that Ireland was the Isle of Man seems daft to us. But in 1846, there was no radar and no form of radio, even. Something else which had also made the *Great Britain* stray off its course was not realised at the time. The iron hull 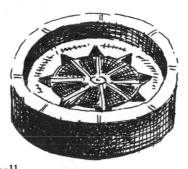 affected the compass very badly. Later, a solution was found for this problem.

Shipwreck in the dark

When the *Great Britain* ran aground, everyone on board was frightened, but unhurt. This showed how much stronger iron steamships were. All through the nineteenth century, we learnt how to do bigger and cleverer things, but great disasters sometimes happened. In 1912 the *Titanic*, the best ship in the world, sank.

Sparks: Historical Adventures

ANCIENT GREECE
The Great Horse of Troy – The Trojan War
0 7496 3369 7 (hbk)   0 7496 3538 X (pbk)
The Winner's Wreath – Ancient Greek Olympics
0 7496 3368 9 (hbk)   0 7496 3555 X (pbk)

INVADERS AND SETTLERS
Boudicca Strikes Back – The Romans in Britain
0 7496 3366 2 (hbk)   0 7496 3546 0 (pbk)
Viking Raiders – A Norse Attack
0 7496 3089 2 (hbk)   0 7496 3457 X (pbk)
Erik's New Home – A Viking Town
0 7496 3367 0 (hbk)   0 7496 3552 5 (pbk)
TALES OF THE ROWDY ROMANS
The Great Necklace Hunt
0 7496 2221 0 (hbk)   0 7496 2628 3 (pbk)
The Lost Legionary
0 7496 2222 9 (hbk)   0 7496 2629 1 (pbk)
The Guard Dog Geese
0 7496 2331 4 (hbk)   0 7496 2630 5 (pbk)
A Runaway Donkey
0 7496 2332 2 (hbk)   0 7496 2631 3 (pbk)

TUDORS AND STUARTS
Captain Drake's Orders – The Armada
0 7496 2556 2 (hbk)   0 7496 3121 X (pbk)
London's Burning – The Great Fire of London
0 7496 2557 0 (hbk)   0 7496 3122 8 (pbk)
Mystery at the Globe – Shakespeare's Theatre
0 7496 3096 5 (hbk)   0 7496 3449 9 (pbk)
Plague! – A Tudor Epidemic
0 7496 3365 4 (hbk)   0 7496 3556 8 (pbk)
Stranger in the Glen – Rob Roy
0 7496 2586 4 (hbk)   0 7496 3123 6 (pbk)
A Dream of Danger – The Massacre of Glencoe
0 7496 2587 2 (hbk)   0 7496 3124 4 (pbk)
A Queen's Promise – Mary Queen of Scots
0 7496 2589 9 (hbk)   0 7496 3125 2 (pbk)
Over the Sea to Skye – Bonnie Prince Charlie
0 7496 2588 0 (hbk)   0 7496 3126 0 (pbk)
TALES OF A TUDOR TEARAWAY
A Pig Called Henry
0 7496 2204 4 (hbk)   0 7496 2625 9 (pbk)
A Horse Called Deathblow
0 7496 2205 9 (hbk)   0 7496 2624 0 (pbk)
Dancing for Captain Drake
0 7496 2234 2 (hbk)   0 7496 2626 7 (pbk)
Birthdays are a Serious Business
0 7496 2235 0 (hbk)   0 7496 2627 5 (pbk)

VICTORIAN ERA
The Runaway Slave – The British Slave Trade
0 7496 3093 0 (hbk)   0 7496 3456 X (pbk)
The Sewer Sleuth – Victorian Cholera
0 7496 2590 2 (hbk)   0 7496 3128 7 (pbk)
Convict! – Criminals Sent to Australia
0 7496 2591 0 (hbk)   0 7496 3129 5 (pbk)
An Indian Adventure – Victorian India
0 7496 3090 6 (hbk)   0 7496 3451 0 (pbk)
Farewell to Ireland – Emigration to America
0 7496 3094 9 (hbk)   0 7496 3448 0 (pbk)

The Great Hunger – Famine in Ireland
0 7496 3095 7 (hbk)   0 7496 3447 2 (pbk)
Fire Down the Pit – A Welsh Mining Disaster
0 7496 3091 4 (hbk)   0 7496 3450 2 (pbk)
Tunnel Rescue – The Great Western Railway
0 7496 3353 0 (hbk)   0 7496 3537 1 (pbk)
Kidnap on the Canal – Victorian Waterways
0 7496 3352 2 (hbk)   0 7496 3540 1 (pbk)
Dr. Barnardo's Boys – Victorian Charity
0 7496 3358 1 (hbk)   0 7496 3541 X (pbk)   ·
The Iron Ship – Brunel's Great Britain
0 7496 3355 7 (hbk)   0 7496 3543 6 (pbk)
Bodies for Sale – Victorian Tomb-Robbers
0 7496 3364 6 (hbk)   0 7496 3539 8 (pbk)
Penny Post Boy – The Victorian Postal Service
0 7496 3362 X (hbk)   0 7496 3544 4 (pbk)
The Canal Diggers – The Manchester Ship Canal
0 7496 3356 5 (hbk)   0 7496 3545 2 (pbk)
The Tay Bridge Tragedy – A Victorian Disaster
0 7496 3354 9 (hbk)   0 7496 3547 9 (pbk)
Stop, Thief! – The Victorian Police
0 7496 3359 X (hbk)   0 7496 3548 7 (pbk)
A School – for Girls! – Victorian Schools
0 7496 3360 3 (hbk)   0 7496 3549 5 (pbk)
Chimney Charlie – Victorian Chimney Sweeps
0 7496 3351 4 (hbk)   0 7496 3551 7 (pbk)
Down the Drain – Victorian Sewers
0 7496 3357 3 (hbk)   0 7496 3550 9 (pbk)
The Ideal Home – A Victorian New Town
0 7496 3361 1 (hbk)   0 7496 3553 3 (pbk)
Stage Struck – Victorian Music Hall
0 7496 3363 8 (hbk)   0 7496 3554 1 (pbk)
TRAVELS OF A YOUNG VICTORIAN
The Golden Key
0 7496 2360 8 (hbk)   0 7496 2632 1 (pbk)
Poppy's Big Push
0 7496 2361 6 (hbk)   0 7496 2633 X (pbk)
Poppy's Secret
0 7496 2374 8 (hbk)   0 7496 2634 8 (pbk)
The Lost Treasure
0 7496 2375 6 (hbk)   0 7496 2635 6 (pbk)

20th-CENTURY HISTORY
Fight for the Vote – The Suffragettes
0 7496 3092 2 (hbk)   0 7496 3452 9 (pbk)
The Road to London – The Jarrow March
0 7496 2609 7 (hbk)   0 7496 3132 5 (pbk)
The Sandbag Secret – The Blitz
0 7496 2608 9 (hbk)   0 7496 3133 3 (pbk)
Sid's War – Evacuation
0 7496 3209 7 (hbk)   0 7496 3445 6 (pbk)
D-Day! – Wartime Adventure
0 7496 3208 9 (hbk)   0 7496 3446 4 (pbk)
The Prisoner – A Prisoner of War
0 7496 3212 7 (hbk)   0 7496 3455 3 (pbk)
Escape from Germany – Wartime Refugees
0 7496 3211 9 (hbk)   0 7496 3454 5 (pbk)
Flying Bombs – Wartime Bomb Disposal
0 7496 3210 0 (hbk)   0 7496 3453 7 (pbk)
12,000 Miles From Home – Sent to Australia
0 7496 3370 0 (hbk)   0 7496 3542 8 (pbk)